SEA KEEPERS

Illustrations by Joanna Kerr and Laura Brett

The Mermaid's Dolphin

Coral Ripley

Contents

Chapter one

The mermaid on the sign had a glittering golden tail, long red hair and a friendly smile. She looked so happy that Emily couldn't help smiling back as she looked up at her.

"The Mermaid Café," Mum read out as she came to stand next to Emily, her arms full of boxes. "I can't believe it's really happening!"

Emily grinned. Her mum had wanted to have her own café for as long as Emily could remember. And when Dad had lost his job a few months ago, the family had decided to move to the seaside and make her dream come true.

"It's beautiful," Emily said to Mum. And it was. All the shops on the old cobblestone road were painted pretty pastel colours – minty green and lemon yellow and sugary pink – but Emily thought the café was the prettiest of all, a pale blue that matched the bit of sea she could see twinkling down at the bottom of the hill. It was so different from the big city they'd lived in before.

"Coming through!" Dad yelled as he staggered over with more boxes. He stopped to plant kisses on both Emily's and Mum's cheeks and then went indoors, whistling. Emily hadn't seen him so cheerful for ages. She was pleased her parents were happy – but she couldn't help feeling sad at the same time. She'd left her school, her friends, everything she knew, back at home. Sandcombe was so pretty, but she didn't know anyone here. How would it ever feel like home? The mermaid on the café sign looked down at her kindly. *It'll all be fine,* she seemed to say. Emily took a deep breath and followed her parents inside.

"Our things go in the flat upstairs, Em, the cooking stuff goes in the kitchen," Mum directed. "I need to start baking and get this café up and running! Just be careful not to let the cat—"

An orange blur streaked down the stairs and ran out the front door.

"Out," Mum finished.

"Sorry!" Dad clattered down the stairs, ducking so he didn't hit his head on the old beam.

"Dad!" Emily exclaimed. "Nemo is meant to stay inside for two weeks so that he can get used to his new home." She couldn't bear it if Nemo got lost. Emily was too little to remember much about when her parents had adopted her as a toddler, but she had always loved animals, so they had promised her a pet when they officially became a family. Nemo was old and grumpy now, but he was still her furry best friend – what if something happened to him?

"I'm sure he'll be fine. I know you still see him as a cute kitten, but he can look after himself. He's probably terrorising some seagulls already," Dad said.

"Shall we go and look for him?" Mum offered.

"It's OK, I'll go," Emily said. "You carry on setting up the café."

"Thanks, darling," Mum said gratefully.

"I'll get his bed ready for when he comes home. And yours as well, I suppose," Dad joked.

The bell dinged as Emily went through the front door and Mum squealed with delight. Emily chuckled, then started to make her way down the cobbled street, towards the seafront.

"Nemo!" she called. She knew Dad was right – Nemo was a big, tough, ginger tomcat – but she still worried about him getting lost. What if he was confused, or scared?

The narrow street opened up to a big harbour filled with boats, and a little sandy beach, curved like a crescent moon. As Emily walked along the harbour wall, she peered behind a stack of lobster traps, keeping her eyes out for a flash of orange fur. A girl about her age and wearing blue dungarees ran up the steps from the beach. Her long dark hair had a red bow in it and she was carrying flip flops. She stopped in front of Emily, her bare feet covered in sand. "Have you lost something?" she asked.

"My cat!" Emily told her. "He's meant to stay indoors for two weeks because we just moved here."

"Oh no!" said the girl, sympathetically. "I've always wanted a cat but my mum's allergic. Don't worry, I'll help you look! I'm sure we'll find him."

"Thank you!" Emily said.

"Where's your new house?" the girl

 15

asked as they continued along the
harbour wall.

"My parents bought a café, the blue
one, up there." Emily pointed.

"Oh wow, that's amazing!" the girl
exclaimed. "I'm Layla. I live up the hill."

"I'm Emily. Thank you so much for
helping."

"It's OK, I was only collecting sea
glass," Layla said as they walked along,
searching for Nemo. She pulled some
smooth, cloudy pieces of sea glass out of
the pocket of her dungarees and showed
them to Emily. "You can get all colours
but red is my favourite."

"Is that really glass?" Emily asked,

admiring the subtle colours of the frosted
glass gems in Layla's hand.

"Glass that's gone into the sea and got
polished," Layla explained, "and then
it washes back up on the beach. It's like
buried treasure!"

Emily smiled. "Mermaid treasure!" she
added. She usually felt nervous talking to
new people, but Layla was so chatty and
friendly she didn't feel awkward at all.

"Oooh, yes, mermaid treasure!" Layla
agreed.

Just then, Emily spotted something
moving in the water. Her heart jumped.
Surely it couldn't be …

Don't be silly! she told herself. *There's*

no such thing as mermaids!

But then there was a splash. "Um, what's that?" she asked Layla.

Layla strained to look out to sea, and then gasped. "I think it's a dolphin."

"Oh, WOW!" Emily cried. She had always wanted to see a real-life dolphin. She'd never thought she'd live so close to them!

"It's swimming really weirdly, though," Layla added. "Come on!" she said, beckoning Emily to follow.

They ran past a fishing boat that was unloading its catch and stopped at the very end of the harbour wall.

"There's definitely something wrong

with it," Layla said, looking worried.

"We have to *do* something," Emily said.

But how could they help the dolphin?

Chapter Two

As Emily tried to think what to do, Layla suddenly started jumping up and down and waving her arms. For a second Emily didn't know what she was doing, but then she noticed a girl with blonde hair on a small boat out on the water.

"Grace! Grace!" Layla yelled.

Emily watched as the girl called Grace steered the dinghy into the harbour. "Are

you OK?" she called up to them.

"Look over there," Layla said, pointing.
"There's something wrong with a
dolphin. We have to help it!"

"Get in," Grace cried, steering her
little boat alongside some steps so the

 22

other two could jump in.

Emily hesitated. She wanted to help but she was meant to be looking for Nemo. Just then she spotted something orange next to a fishing boat moored up in the harbour. It was Nemo! As Emily watched, one of the men threw him a fish, and another scratched him behind the ears. Dad was right, Nemo had made himself at home right away!

Emily and Layla jumped down into the dinghy and Grace handed them both life jackets.

"Hi," Emily said, shyly.

"This is Emily. She just moved into the blue café," Layla chattered. "Grace has lived here forever. She's brilliant with boats because her grandad's a fisherman.

We'll all be in the same class at school!"

"We might not be," Emily said. At her old school, there had been three classes for every year group. But it would be amazing if they *were* all in the same class, then she would know someone on the first day of school …

To her surprise, Grace grinned. "We definitely will! There's only one class for our year," she told Emily.

"You can sit next to me," Layla promised. Emily's heart jumped happily. Suddenly, lots of her worries about going to a new school vanished.

Grace gunned the engine and the dinghy sped along the waves. The wind whipped Emily's hair and she breathed in the sea air excitedly. But she couldn't stop worrying about the poor dolphin. As they got closer, Emily could see his sleek grey body, dragging something along behind him as he struggled to swim.

"It's caught in a net!" Layla gasped.

Grace slowly steered the boat close to the dolphin, then switched off the engine so the sound didn't frighten him.

As the dolphin twisted, Emily could see his fin tangled in the net. "We have to help!" she said.

Grace started taking off her shoes. She looked like she was going to jump in!

Emily grabbed her arm before she

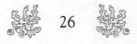

could. "Be careful," she told her, "wild animals can be dangerous if they're hurt and scared."

"Good point." Grace nodded. She grabbed the trailing end of the net, but the dolphin just thrashed more wildly,

 27

spraying the girls with water, and
rocking the dinghy. "I can't untangle it
like this!" she cried.

"We have to do *something*," said Emily.
She racked her brains for everything
she knew about dolphins. They ate fish,
they lived in groups called pods, they
liked singing to each other ... "Maybe
we should sing to the dolphin to soothe
him," she suggested.

"It's worth a try," said Grace. "But my
voice is rubbish."

"Ooh! I love singing!" said Layla.
"I'm in the school choir." She instantly
launched into *Twinkle, Twinkle, Little
Star.*

To Emily's amazement, the dolphin stopped thrashing. "We're going to get you out, just hold still," Emily said softly, trying to keep him calm.

As Layla continued singing – moving on to *Happy Birthday* – Emily and Grace reached over the side of the boat and started tugging the net away from the dolphin's fin. The dolphin seemed to like Layla's sweet, clear voice, staying still as he listened.

"Got it!" Emily said eventually, tugging the last piece of tangled net away from the dolphin's fin and then collapsing into the dinghy. Finally, the dolphin was free! Layla stopped singing and helped

Emily and Grace haul the net into the dinghy. The dolphin looked at them for a moment, then seemed to realise he wasn't tangled any more. With an excited click, he flipped his tail and swam around the boat, splashing and squealing, then he dived and disappeared into the green depths. The girls laughed in delight.

"Where did you learn about dolphins?" Grace asked Emily.

She shrugged. "I watch a lot of nature programmes on TV. I love animals. But it was Layla's singing that did the trick."

"It was your idea," said Layla. She smiled at the others. "The three of us make a good team."

 30

Emily looked at the net coiled in the
bottom of the dinghy. It was slimy with
green seaweed and it smelt horrible!

"The dolphin would have died if we
hadn't been able to free him," Grace said
grimly. "My grandad would never leave

 31

a net in the sea like this."

There was a splash of water behind them. The dolphin was back! He circled round and round, sped away a short distance, then came straight back to the dinghy. Then he did it again, and again as the girls watched, curiously.

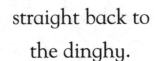

Emily shook her head. It was as if the dolphin was trying to tell them something.

"This might sound crazy …" Layla said.

"But I think he wants us to follow him!"

"I think you're right," Grace said slowly. "My dog Barkley acts like that sometimes."

Emily looked at the dolphin's wide grin. "Do you want us to follow you?" she asked. The dolphin seemed to nod, then spun around and swam off.

"Follow that dolphin!" yelled Layla.

Grace turned on the engine and they raced after the flashing fins. A couple of times they almost lost sight of him, but both times the dolphin popped his head out of the water, looking back at them and clicking as if he was telling them to hurry up.

The dolphin led them towards the cliffs, then disappeared under the waves.

"Oh," Emily said, feeling disappointed. "Maybe he *wasn't* trying to lead us somewhere." After all, dolphins couldn't really understand people. But she'd been so sure …

"Look, there's the dolphin again!" Grace said, pointing.

The dolphin was at the entrance of a cave. Grace started steering the boat towards it.

"Is it safe to go in there?" asked Emily nervously.

Grace nodded. "The tide's going out, so we'll be fine." She turned off the engine

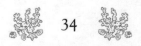

34

and they used the paddles to manoeuvre the dinghy into the cave. At first it was small and dark, but then it opened up into a huge cavern, filled with sparkling aquamarine water. Emily gasped, and

next to her she heard Grace and Layla do the same. It was so beautiful!

There was a small, sandy beach on one side, so they paddled over and jumped out, splashing though the water as they pulled the dinghy up onto the shore.

"I never knew this was here," Grace said.

"It's a secret cave!" Layla breathed.

"Not so secret any more," said a voice from the water.

The girls turned. There, in the middle of the aquamarine pool, was the dolphin. And hugging him was a girl with the brightest, most beautiful hair Emily had ever seen. The girl smiled and waved at

them, her pink and purple hair tumbling over her shoulders. Then she dived under and a moment later a glittering lilac-coloured tail flipped out of the water.

Emily felt her eyes widen. The girl was a real-live mermaid!

Chapter Three

The mermaid popped her head above the water again. "Thank you for rescuing Kai," she said, stroking the dolphin's nose. "He's my best friend. With all the awful stuff happening at home, I couldn't bear to lose him too."

Emily looked at Layla, but for once her chatty new friend seemed lost for words. "You're welcome," Emily said. "I'm really sorry he got caught in a net."

"You're a mermaid!" Layla blurted.

"My grandad always said mermaids were real," Grace told her. "I don't think he's ever met one, though."

The mermaid laughed. "Well, we usually try to stay hidden from humans.

But Kai thought that you would be able to help. I'm Marina, by the way, and this is Kai."

"I'm Layla," said Layla, "and this is Emily and Grace."

"We definitely will help, if we can," Emily told her.

Kai swam over to Emily, his mouth open wide in a cheeky grin. Then he turned and clicked at Marina.

The mermaid screwed up her nose and twisted a strand of her purple hair around her finger. "I don't know ..." she said hesitantly.

Kai clicked again and smacked his tail on the water.

"I don't know what he said, but I agree with the dolphin," Layla joked.

Marina nodded her head. "OK!" she said. "This is totally against the rules … are you really sure you want to help?" she asked, looking at them intently.

"Yes!" Grace and Layla replied right away.

Emily paused. The other two girls looked at her. "I do want to help, I really do," she said desperately, "but I'm meant to be unpacking, we just got here and there's so much to do …" She trailed off. She didn't want to sound babyish, but she knew her parents would be worried about her if she wasn't back soon.

Marina gave a kind smile that reminded Emily of the mermaid on the café sign. "Don't worry, no time will pass in the human world while you're with me," she told them. "It's part of the mermaid magic."

Emily let out a breath. She could stay after all! "Great!" she said, grinning. "In that case, let's go!"

"Come into the water!" Marina called. Holding hands, the girls stepped into the sea.

Marina began to sing in a beautiful high voice:

"Water magic, waves and swirls,
Use your power upon these girls.

Let them dive down deep with me,
And visit my home beneath the sea."

Emily felt a strange whooshing
sensation, like she was tumbling in the
water, turning over and over and over
again. Then as suddenly as it had started,
it stopped.

Emily opened her eyes. She was completely underwater, her hair floating around her head, but she could breathe as easily as if she was still up on the beach.

"Whoa," Layla's voice came from next to her. "That was weird. I felt like I was in a washing machine."

"Are you guys OK?" Grace asked.

"I think so," Emily said. She could talk underwater, too! Layla was floating next to her, rubbing her eyes ... and swishing her bright turquoise tail.

"Oh, wow!" Grace yelled.

Emily glanced to her other side and saw Grace doing underwater flips, her

 45

long pink tail spinning her around and around.

Emily looked down and gasped. Where her legs usually were, there was a gorgeous, sparkling yellow tail. It was covered in tiny golden scales, the size of her littlest fingernail. At the end, where her feet should have been, were two broad fins. She wriggled her toes and her fins flipped. This was amazing!

Grace swam over and grabbed her hand, then Emily reached out for Layla. The three girls held hands and swam round and round in delight.

"I can't believe it!" Emily laughed as they spun, getting used to their tails.

"We're actually mermaids!"

Marina laughed too as she and Kai swam over to them. Close up, her tail shimmered with all different shades of purple. Marina gave Layla a hug while Kai nudged Emily with his nose.

"Hi," she said softly.

"Hi!" Kai clicked back. "Thank you for rescuing me!"

"I can understand you!" Emily exclaimed.

"It's probably because you're a mermaid!" Layla joked, nudging her with her fin.

"I know, I just can't believe it! I've always wanted to be able to talk to animals!" Emily cried.

Grace was stretching her tail. "How fast can we go?" she asked. "I'm the fastest swimmer on my team but I bet I can beat my record with this!"

Layla pulled a silly face. "Bleurgh, I don't want to go fast, I get seasick."

"Can mermaids even *get* seasick?" Emily wondered aloud.

Marina laughed. "I'll answer all your questions," she said. "But first, come with me." She turned, flipped her tail, and shot off through the water. The girls glanced at her then followed, Kai excitedly swimming circles around them.

"We're going to Atlantis, my home,"

 49

Marina told them as they swam. "My parents are King Caspian and Queen Adrianna."

"That must make you—" Layla started.

"Princess Marina of Atlantis!" Marina stuck out her tongue and giggled as she spun around, her pinky-purple hair fanning out through the water.

Emily grinned. She hadn't just met a mermaid, but a mermaid princess!

"It's our job to look after all sea creatures," Marina said. She stopped and looked at them, suddenly serious. "But it's getting harder and harder. There are just too many problems. Humans have put so much pollution and rubbish in the sea, and it's hurting the sea creatures. There just aren't enough mermaids to help them all. It makes me so angry." Marina twitched her tail crossly.

"I'm sorry," Emily whispered.

"We have to stop it," Layla said fiercely.

Grace nodded. "What can we do to help?"

Marina sighed. "Unfortunately, humans aren't the only problem we have at the moment. Let's go through and I'll explain everything."

Emily looked around, confused. "Go through what?" The water around them was empty apart from a column of

bubbles rising from the seabed.

"Atlantis is hidden by powerful mermaid magic," Marina explained. "But the entrance is right here!" She swam though the bubbles, and suddenly disappeared.

The girls looked at one another excitedly.

"What are we waiting for? Come on!" Grace said. Grinning, she swam through the bubbles and vanished from sight.

Emily hesitated.

"Let's go through together," Layla suggested.

Emily nodded, her tummy flipping nervously.

Layla grabbed Emily's hand and
together they kicked their tails and
swam forward, bubbles popping and
fizzing all around them. As the magical

bubbles cleared, Emily rubbed her eyes in astonishment as she stared at amazing sight in front of her.

"Oh, WOW!" she breathed.

Chapter Four

Everywhere Emily looked there were hundreds of mermaids, with tails all colours of the rainbow. As the girls watched, two beautiful white-haired and golden-tailed mermaids passed by, riding in a pearl carriage pulled by two huge seahorses. Nearby, an orange-tailed mermaid with black hair held onto the fin of an orca. There were creatures

Emily had only seen on TV programmes about sea life – and lots that she'd never seen before. And they were all heading towards a shimmering, sparkling palace made of seashells and coral.

"Welcome to Atlantis!" Marina said with a grin. "It isn't always this busy," she told them as they watched the merfolk swimming towards the palace. The girls gasped as a huge humpback whale swam overhead and then dived down. It was carrying several merpeople on its back, like an underwater bus!

"Merfolk are gathering from across the seven seas so that a Sea Keeper can be chosen," Marina told them. She sighed again, and sat on the top of a rock, flipping her fins sadly. Kai swam over and nuzzled under her arm.

"There hasn't been a Sea Keeper for hundreds of years," Marina explained, "not since the great battle between merfolk and sirens."

"What's a siren—" Emily started to ask, but just then there was a loud trumpeting noise.

"The ceremony!" Marina sprang up. "Quick!"

She swam towards the palace and the girls followed as fast as their fins would carry them. All the merfolk were gathering in the main courtyard, talking worriedly among themselves.

"There are my parents." Marina pointed to a mermaid couple swimming above the crowd.

I would have known they were the king and queen even if Marina hadn't told

me, Emily thought to herself. Marina's mum had a regal red tail and blue hair, and was waving to the crowd. King Caspian had a blue tail, green hair and a beard. They were both wearing crowns made out of plaited seaweed and pearls.

There was a hush in the crowd as Queen Adrianna swam forward to speak. "Friends! Thank you for gathering here today. These are troubling times, and I am sad to say that the rumours are true: a siren has returned to our waters. Effluvia, the worst of them all, is back, and she has vowed to release all her siren sisters and take over Atlantis, for ever!"

A gasp rippled across the watching

merfolk. Queen Adrianna raised her hand.

"But do not fear, because in times of need, heroes rise. We are here today to select a new Sea Keeper!"

This time, a cheer rose up from the merfolk.

"It is a great honour to be chosen as a Sea Keeper, but it is a dangerous task, so let any who do not wish to be chosen leave the palace now," Queen Adrianna announced. Behind them, a mermaid hustled her children out. A few others left, but most remained.

"Sirens are a type of mermaid with a really powerful song," Marina explained to the girls in a whisper. "They can use it to hypnotise people into doing what they want. They tried to steal the Golden Pearls and use their magic to take over Atlantis, until my ancestor, Queen Nerissa, banished them. The sirens were sent to the deepest depths of the ocean, and the pearls were scattered in hiding places across the corners of the seven seas to protect them. No one knows how Effluvia escaped, but now she's back and she's causing trouble for us merfolk. She wants a Golden Pearl so she can use its magical power to free her sisters. That would spell disaster for the merpeople and the oceans we protect. We can't let that happen. The Sea Keepers *have* to find the pearls before she does."

Emily glanced at Grace and Layla. They looked as concerned as she felt.

Marina pointed to a tall, green-haired merman at the front, who was laughing loudly and jostling his two friends. "My older brother, Prince Neptune, thinks he'll be the new Sea Keeper. And he probably will be," she added glumly. "What Neptune wants, he

usually gets." She
rolled her eyes.

"Silence, please!"
Queen Adrianna held
her arms out wide,
then started to sing
in a breathtakingly
beautiful voice.

**"Water magic,
hear my plea,
A new Sea Keeper,
reveal to me ..."**

As Adrianna sang,
the water around
her swirled like a
whirlpool. When the

magical bubbles cleared, three sparkling purple shells appeared, spinning gently overhead.

"There must be three Sea Keepers this time!" Marina whispered.

Prince Neptune and his friends looked smug as the shells floated towards them. But to their surprise, the shells didn't stop.

"Hey, where are you going?" the prince shouted as the shells passed over his head.

"Where *are* they going?" wondered Marina aloud as the three sparkling shells floated towards the back of the courtyard.

   65

The crowd turned as the shells floated right to the back and stopped above Emily, Grace and Layla's heads.

"What's going on?" Emily whispered to Marina. Every single mermaid and

merman was staring at them.

Marina looked pale. "The magic has chosen the new Sea Keepers …" she said. "And it's the three of you!"

Emily looked up at the sparkling shell hovering above her head, matching the ones floating over Grace and Layla.

"This is amazing!" Layla whispered, waving excitedly to all the mermaids.

But not everyone seemed happy. At the front, Prince Neptune turned huffily and swam into the palace.

"What does it mean?" Grace asked.

Before Marina could explain, the crowd of merfolk parted and Queen Adrianna and King Caspian swam up to them.

 67

"Marina, who are your new friends?"
Queen Adrianna said, eyeing the girls
suspiciously.

"I can explain—" Marina started.

Queen Adrianna gave her daughter a stern look, then turned and addressed the crowd. "The Sea Keepers have been chosen!" she cried. The watching merfolk gave a great cheer. "Soon they will find the Golden Pearls and protect the oceans and seas from Effluvia's wicked sorcery. I urge you to help them as much as you can on their journey. But now, we must prepare. The fate of our world depends on it."

"Mama—" Marina whispered, but the queen flicked her fins and swept past them, heading back into the palace.

Emily still wasn't sure if mermaids

could get seasick, but Marina definitely looked queasy. "Are you OK?" she asked.

"Not really," Marina muttered to the girls. "I am in soooo much trouble!"

Chapter Five

Emily squeezed the mermaid's hand and Marina smiled gratefully. Then she swam after her parents, the girls trailing behind them .

The great palace doors, made of two enormous white shells, had barely closed when Queen Adrianna shouted, "They're human, aren't they? I can sense your magic all over them."

King Capsian gasped. He came forward and looked them up and down, his long green beard swaying in the water like

seaweed. "Are you human?" he asked gently.

Layla nodded. "We just want to help, Your Majesty."

"It's not Marina's fault," Emily added.

"We're *good* humans," Grace tried to tell them,

but the royal mermaids were too cross to listen.

Prince Neptune swam over to them. "Wow, you've really done it this time, sis," he said mockingly.

"Humans are AWFUL!" Queen Adrianna shook her head at Marina. "I can't believe you've brought some here, to our home. They pollute the oceans, catch the fish, kill whales for FUN ... they're almost as bad as sirens."

Marina looked like she was about to cry. Kai went to her side and nuzzled her shoulder.

"What were you thinking?" King Caspian asked.

 73

"Something has to be done!" Marina said, wiping tears away fiercely. "We can't just watch the oceans dying. We have to do something. And these human girls are different, I know they are. They saved Kai's life … maybe they could save us too."

Prince Neptune scoffed.

Queen Adrianna studied each girl in turn. Emily looked back at her. *Please,* she thought as hard as she could. *Please let us help.*

Queen Adrianna seemed to make a decision. "For whatever reason, the water magic has chosen you to become our Sea Keepers," she said, sighing. "We will

have to trust the magic and put our faith
in you. Will you make the Sea Keeper
vow?"

"Oh, yes!" Layla exclaimed.

Grace gave a nod.

Emily felt her tummy churning nervously, but she nodded too.

"Repeat after me." The queen started to sing again, her beautiful voice swirling though the water like liquid silver.

"I promise to protect all
who live in the sea,
From sharks, skates
and squid, to anemones.
The Golden Pearls I promise to find,
To use their power for mermaid kind.
I'll honour the oceans, from shore to shore,
And be a Sea Keeper for ever more."

The girls repeated the promise. "… for ever more," they finished together.

Queen Adrianna held up her hand.
The water shimmered and swirled with
colourful magic and the three purple
shells, still floating above the girls,
transformed into beautiful shell bracelets
on each of their wrists. "These magic
bracelets will let you become mermaids
whenever you need to be. And my
daughter will help you on your mission to
bring back the pearls."

"But, Mama, I'm not a Sea Keeper—"
Marina started.

Queen Adrianna raised her hand and
Marina stopped talking.

"You brought these girls here and they
have become our Sea Keepers. But they

  77

do not know our world. You must go with them," the queen said firmly.

"Good luck, my daughter," King Caspian said.

As her parents swam away, Marina let out a deep breath. "Maybe I *did* do the right thing bringing you here …"

 78

Prince Neptune snorted. "Yeah, right, as if some two-legs could help us. All they do is hurt our world." He glared at the girls, then flipped over and swished his tail in their faces. "Oh, and before you go congratulating yourselves, you still have to meet the Mystic Clam," Prince Neptune called over his shoulder. "Good luck. You're going to need it." His mocking laughter echoed through the palace as he swam away.

"Um, who's the Mystic Clam?" Layla asked.

Marina suddenly looked nervous again. "You'd better come with me," she said, leading them through the corridors

of the palace, past intricately woven
seaweed tapestries on the walls and
ceilings covered with all kinds of shells
in beautiful patterns. She swam up to a
huge mussel-shell door and stopped. "The
Mystic Clam is older than the palace,"
she said in a half whisper. "He's been
asleep for hundreds of years, but last
week—"

"Who goes there?" a deep voice called
from inside the room.

"He woke up!" Marina whispered.

"You may enter," the voice called.

Layla gasped. Emily's tummy jumped
nervously.

"OK, let's meet this clam and find out

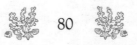

what happens next," Grace said bravely.
Marina opened the door and Grace swam
in first.

Layla grabbed Emily's hand, and Emily

squeezed hers back as they followed the other two inside.

The room was dimly lit by glowing starfish. In the middle was a gigantic clam, bigger than a table, covered in barnacles and seaweed.

"Um, hello!" Layla said, like it was normal to be talking to a giant mollusc.

The Mystic Clam's shell creaked open a crack. "Hello, Princess Marina. Hello, humans."

"How did you know we're human?" Grace asked.

"I am mystical, you know," the clam said, bits of seaweed swaying in the water as it spoke. "Also Queen Adrianna's

voice is very loud, and sound carries well in water." The clam gave a rumbling noise which Emily guessed was a laugh.

"You're not cross that we're the Sea Keepers?" Layla asked.

 83

The clam rumbled again. "All is as it should be," it said.

"Phew. So you're not going to, like, eat us," Layla said in relief.

"You thought he was going to eat you?" Marina whispered.

"I don't know what clams eat!" Layla replied.

"Well, they don't eat people!" Emily told her. The clam gave his rumbling laugh again.

Grace swam forward. "We need to find these Golden Pearls, right? Can you tell us where they are?" she asked.

"It's been such a long time ... hundreds and hundred of years ..." The clam's

voice faded away. Then little noises
started coming out of its shell.

"Is … is he … snoring?" Emily
whispered to her friends.

Layla giggled.

"Come on!"
Grace told them.
"It's important."

"Sorry. Um,
Mystic Clam?"
Emily asked,
tapping gently
on the huge,
barnacle-topped
shell.

The clam woke

 85

up with a start. "Where was I?"

"You have to tell us where the Golden Pearls are," Emily reminded him gently, "so that we can find them and stop Effluvia freeing her siren sisters."

"Ah yes," the clam replied. "There's just one problem. I can't remember where they are. There were so many, and it was so long ago ..."

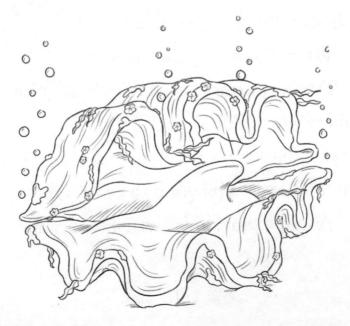

The girls looked at each other in dismay. If the clam couldn't help, then how would they ever find the pearls?

Emily stroked the old shell gently. "It's OK," she said. "Why don't you tell us what you *do* remember?"

The clam creaked open. "Queen Nerissa cast the pearls far and wide, shallow and deep. There was one ..." The clam lapsed into silence.

"Where?" Grace said eagerly.

"Don't interrupt," said the clam. "Now, where was I? Ah, yes ..." The clam announced in a rumbling voice:

"Deep in a forest, lush and green,
A magic pearl hides its golden gleam.

It lies in wait on a sandy seabed,
Where once a human lost her head."

Emily shivered. That sounded scary.

"Is that it?" Grace muttered.

"Shhhh." Layla nudged her friend.

But the clam opened his shell in a great yawn. "Now, if you don't mind, I'm going to have a nap. It's hard work being mystic, and I am very, very old."

Marina and the girls turned to go, but before they left the room, the clam spoke once more.

"Good luck, Sea Keepers. The future of our world depends on you."

Chapter Six

Emily, Grace, Layla and Marina swam out of the room quietly. Kai was waiting for them outside.

"Did you find out where the pearls are?" the dolphin clicked anxiously.

"Not exactly …" Emily said.

"Why didn't the clam just tell us?" Grace said in frustration. "Why did he have to make it so difficult?"

Marina shrugged. "He's mystic, so he works in mysterious ways."

"But we still don't know *anything*." Layla sighed. "I don't even know what the pearls do ..."

"Oh, I know that," Marina said. "The pearls are magic. Each one has the power to grant a wish."

"What did the riddle mean?" Emily wondered aloud. "*Deep in a forest ...*"

"Any ideas?" Grace asked hopefully.

Marina shook her head.

"It must mean a seaweed forest, right?" Grace said practically. "I mean, there aren't trees underwater."

Kai gave a loud click. "I know a place

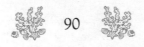

90

where the seaweed almost reaches the water's surface," he told them, swimming round excitedly. "Could that be where the pearl is?"

"Let's find out!" Emily said, her heart pounding with anticipation.

Leaving the palace, they set off, Kai leading the way though the water. As they swam, they passed beautiful anemones, scuttling crabs and brightly

coloured sea sponges.

"Look!" Grace gasped as a huge turtle appeared from the ocean floor and swam past them.

Emily couldn't tear her eyes away from the greens and browns of its skin and shell as it swam through the sunshine that was dancing in the water. It was so amazing!

"Hello, Sea Keepers!" called the turtle.

Emily smiled in delight. The turtle knew who they were!

"News travels fast underwater," Marina said with a grin.

"The seaweed forest is up ahead, just past these rocks," Kai said, racing ahead.

"Wait for us, dolphins are faster than mermaids!" Layla said, laughing.

"I bet I can swim as fast as a dolphin," Grace said.

"You're on!" Kai clicked.

As Kai and Grace flipped their tails and sped off, they were surrounded by a huge school of tiny silver sardines. There were hundreds of them, flashing and rushing, dipping and darting in a great cloud of fish.

Emily laughed as they surrounded her – they seemed to be having so much fun. But then she heard their high-pitched voices calling out, "Sea Ghost! Sea Ghost!" The tiny sardines rushed past

the girls like a quick-flowing silver river. Emily realised they weren't having fun, they were frightened. "Swim!" their little voices called out. "Swim for your lives!"

Then, as quick as they'd come, the sardines disappeared.

"Are you OK?" Grace yelled.

"I've been squashed like a sardine before, but never *by* a sardine!" Layla joked.

"Those fish were so scared," Emily said. "What's a sea ghost?"

"I have no idea." Marina shook her head.

Swimming towards them was a baby dolphin. Emily's heart leapt at the sight of it, and Layla squealed out loud. "Awww, it's so cute!"

But there was something wrong. The baby was all on his own, and he wasn't playfully leaping and having fun – he

was swimming away in fear, just like the sardines!

"I know we have to find the pearl, but I think that baby dolphin needs our help," said Layla.

"We did promise to protect all who live in the sea," said Emily.

She glanced at her friends and could see they were thinking the same thing.

Layla gave a nod.

"Come on!" Grace called.

They swam over to the terrified dolphin as fast as their fins could carry them. Kai sped ahead clicking in concern.

"He's called Splash," he told the girls and Marina as they approached. They

surrounded the baby dolphin, who looked up at them anxiously.

"What's wrong, Splash?" Emily asked gently.

"Where's your family?" Layla added.

"I got lost," Splash clicked. "We were swimming away from the ghost and I went the wrong way. It nearly ate me!" Splash pointed a fin and gave a squeal of alarm. "The ghost – it's coming!"

Emily held her breath as she saw a huge, dark shadow coming towards them. It was floating in the mouth of the cove, and was green and thick with seaweed. It didn't look like any animal she could think of, and it didn't seem to

 98

be swimming towards them, just moving
with the waves … As the ghost moved
closer Splash whimpered and Kai tucked
him under his fin.

"Don't worry, we won't let it get

you." Marina bravely swam in front of
the baby dolphin, stretching her arms
out to protect Splash.

Emily, Grace and
Layla joined
her, forming
a barrier.
The shadow
got closer
and closer,
looming over them
menacingly. The seas
went dark as it blocked out the light.

"I want my mama!" Splash said.

"Don't worry, we'll help you find your
family," Emily promised.

"Let's get out of here," Layla said.

But Grace was still studying the monster. "Hang on," she said.

"Grace, no!" Layla shouted, but it was too late, Grace was already swimming towards the creature. The ghost moved, flapping a great wing towards her – and Grace vanished from sight.

"It's eaten her!" the baby dolphin squeaked.

"Grace!" Emily yelled.

"It's OK!" Grace called back. "It's just a net!"

Emily felt a surge of relief, until she got closer to the net and saw it properly. It was full of decaying fish and other sea creatures. Crabs were crawling over it, eating the rotting creatures. It made her feel sick.

"Eugh, gross!" Layla exclaimed. "And it stinks!"

Marina and the dolphins could hardly bear to look.

"This is what happens when fishermen lose their nets," Grace said, trying to gather up the net and hold her nose at the same time. "They're called ghost nets. They stay underwater, doing what they're made for – catching fish. They just float along, killing more and more creatures."

Emily was horrified. There was the net

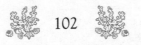

that had caught Kai this morning, and
now this one. How many ghost nets were
out there?

"At least we can stop this one," Grace
said determinedly. She caught armfuls
of the floating net, trying to avoid the

 103

disgusting bits, and swam over to some nearby rocks, jutting up from the seabed. She lifted one of the smaller ones and used it to pin down the net. Emily, Layla and Marina went to help. The crabs had scurried away as the net moved, but they came back and swarmed all over it.

"Please be careful," Marina said, moving her hands like pincers as she spoke to them. The crabs nodded, and scuttled away.

Marina, Emily, Layla and Grace worked together to pin the net down under the rocks. Finally it was covered. It couldn't hurt anyone else.

"Now we can help Splash find his

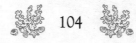

family," Emily said happily.

"Our first day as Sea Keepers and we've already defeated a monster!" Layla joked.

"Go, Sea Keepers!" Grace whooped.

"Oh, I wouldn't celebrate just yet," a voice came from behind them.

The girls turned to see a tall mermaid with long midnight-blue hair, a dark purple tail and an icy gleam in her eyes.

"Effluvia!" Marina said with a gasp.

 106

Chapter Seven

Effluvia gave a cruel smile. "I see you know who I am," she said. "And this is my little pet, Fang." She pointed to a small, round fish with sharp fangs and a light dangling in front of its face. "But aren't you going to introduce yourselves?" Her voice was soft and lilting, but her tail flicked angrily.

That's what Nemo does before he

pounces, Emily thought to herself.

Marina swam forward bravely. "I am Princess Marina of Atlantis," she said, swimming in front of Effluvia and raising herself as tall as she could on her purple tail.

"Nice to meet you, Your Royal Highness!" Effluvia gave a mocking bow. Now Grace swam

 108

forward. "And we're the Sea Keepers," she said, looking Effluvia right in the eye.

"So, you're the mermaids that are going to stop me from getting the Golden Pearls, are you?" She stopped and looked at them closely. "But you're not mermaids, are you?" she said slowly.

The siren swam past Marina, Fang bobbing after her, and inspected Emily, Layla and Grace from their heads to their fins.

"You're human girls! This is who they send to defeat me?" She gave a laugh that sounded beautiful, like tinkling bells, but still sent chills down Emily's spine. Layla squeezed her hand reassuringly.

"Get away from them!" Marina called out.

Effluvia pointed her finger and let out a high note, like an opera singer. The girls watched in horror as the ghost net twitched and rose up, pulling free from the huge pile of rocks, before twisting around Marina. The mermaid struggled against it, but the net held her tight.

Effluvia smiled nastily and turned back to the girls. "Now, I know you don't want any trouble. You're not even from the sea, this isn't your fight. Tell me what I want to know and I'll let you go. I'll even send you back to shore, now wouldn't that be nice? Then you can be among all the other *two-legs*" – she spat the word out – "and leave the mermaid world to me. So I'll ask you nicely: where are the Golden Pearls?"

Emily shook her head. Next to her, Grace did the same.

"We don't know!" Layla burst out.

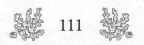

"And even if we did, we'd never tell you!"

"Fine," Effluvia snapped. "We'll do it the hard way."

She took a deep breath, and Emily shut her eyes, half expecting her to breathe fire or shout at them.

Instead she stared directly at the girls and started to sing … and it was the most strange and wonderful thing Emily had ever heard.

She couldn't make out the words, but
she felt the music with her whole body,
as the song flooded her mind. It was
mesmerising and magical, and it made
Emily feel that Effluvia was beautiful and
good and kind. Emily knew she had to
help her and tell her everything she knew
about the Golden Pearls ...

 113

Faintly in the distance she could hear Marina shouting. "Don't listen, it's a siren song! She's putting you under her spell!" But the words didn't seem to make any sense.

"Now tell me," Effluvia said, fixing the girls with her stare, "where is the Golden Pearl?"

"The seaweed for—" Emily started to say.

"Argh!" screamed Effluvia. Kai had charged into the siren, swooshing his tail and sending her spinning off though the water. Then he and Splash swam over to Marina and bit the net, pulling it open enough for

Marina to wriggle free.

"Wake up!" Marina yelled, swimming over to the girls and shaking them one by one.

Emily felt like she'd been asleep, having wonderful dreams. Next to her

Grace was rubbing her eyes and Layla
still looked groggy. "Oh no!" Emily
gasped, putting her hands to her mouth.
"Did we tell her anything about the
pearl?"

Marina shook her head. "Nearly, but
Kai distracted Effluvia and broke the
spell."

"Get away, you overgrown sprat!"
Effluvia was thrashing her tail at Kai,
who was now circling round her.

"That was close!" Marina said.
"Another few minutes and you'd have
been totally under her control."

"What *was* that?" Grace asked.

Emily shook her head. It felt fuzzy, like

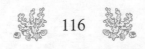

she'd been up late and eaten too many sweets at a sleepover.

"Her siren song," Marina explained. "All mermaid magic is sung, but sirens have a particularly powerful song, and they use it to control. That's why they're so dangerous – they can make you do whatever they want."

Effluvia's laugh rippled through the water as she swam up to them. "Don't think you'll beat me that easily, Sea Keepers," she said, her lilting voice turning into a snarl. "I know there must be a pearl around here somewhere, otherwise why would you be here?"

Fang hid behind Effluvia's tail and

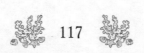

stuck his tongue
out at them.
"We're
not scared
of you,
Effluvia,"
Grace said.

Emily was, but she
wasn't going to let that stop her. She was
a Sea Keeper, and she was determined to
get that pearl!

Effluvia waved her hands in the water
and let out another beautiful song. The
girls instantly clamped their hands over
their ears to block out the sound.

Effluvia laughed and turned away from

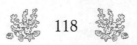

them. "This one isn't for you, two-legs," she told them. "I have bigger fish to fry."

She sang again, and from behind the rocks something appeared … stirring the water. A long tentacle, covered with hundreds of suckers, then another and another.

Emily watched in disbelief as the enormous creature appeared behind Effluvia. It had a huge cone-shaped head and eight thick tentacles, covered in hundreds of round suckers the size of dinner plates. The creature's skin was white and coral-red. It would have been beautiful if it weren't so scary!

"What is that?" Layla whispered.

"I have no idea," Grace replied.

"I think it's a giant squid," Emily told them.

"It's definitely a giant," Layla said with a gulp.

"I don't know what she's doing here," Marina told them, "Squid live in the deepest part of the sea, where they can grow to be enormous. This one's only young."

"They get bigger?" Layla squeaked.

The squid spread out her tentacles. Then at a nod from Effluvia, she started to whip up the water. The water swirled and churned until Emily was struggling to swim. It was like walking up a hill on a very windy day; she had to lean into the water and push her tail as hard as she could just so she wasn't swept away.

Effluvia laughed louder as the water became so cloudy with churned-up sand

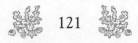

121

that Emily couldn't see more than a few centimetres in front of her.

"Hold on!" Marina yelled out. The girls all grabbed hands and Emily hugged Splash tight to keep him safe from the rough swells.

The squid was churning up a sea storm!

Chapter Eight

"Quick, behind the rocks," Grace yelled. They managed to swim over and duck down behind the pile of rocks, where the water was calmer. They all breathed sighs of relief.

"Are you OK, Splash?" Emily asked, stroking the baby dolphin's smooth skin.

"I want my mama," the little dolphin sniffled.

 123

"We can't find your family OR the pearl while the water is rough like this," Grace said, thinking out loud. "First we have to stop the squid."

"Mermaids protect all sea creatures," Marina said. "Whatever we do we can't hurt her."

Emily shook her head. She didn't want to harm the squid either. Kai had broken the spell on them by distracting Effluvia, but now the siren was nowhere in sight. Maybe they could distract the squid in the same way? "Can we talk to her?" she asked.

"It's worth a try!" Marina said.

"Kai, can you stay with Splash?" Emily asked.

Kai nodded his head. Leaving the two dolphins sheltering behind the rock, they headed back towards the squid. It was hard work swimming against the strong current. There was no sign of Effluvia or Fang, but the squid was still there, stirring up the water with her enormous tentacles. Emily gasped as she saw the squid up close again. She was so huge! How were they ever going to stop her?

"Mighty squid!" Marina called up at her. But with one flick of a tentacle the squid channelled a gush of water which sent the mermaid princess flying off through the water. Grace tried next, dodging past thrashing tentacles as she tried to get its attention. "Hey, squid! Over here!"

"Please, Miss Squid, we just want to talk," Layla said, ducking out of the way as a tentacle smashed down on the seabed.

"Please, just listen!" Emily called out, swimming as close as she dared to the creature's great cone-shaped head. The squid just blinked its great eye and lashed the water even harder.

"This is no good," Grace said as they all gathered together, sheltering back behind the rocks.

"I have an idea," Marina said. She closed her eyes and waved her hands in the water. Bright colours swirled

around her fingertips. Emily felt a thrill
of excitement – Marina was going to do
mermaid magic again!

"Water magic, wave and tide,
Show us how the squid feels inside."

Suddenly Emily could hear something
in her mind, like she was listening to a
voice on her earphones.

MY HOME, MY BEAUTIFUL HOME,
a deep voice wailed.

"It's the squid," Marina said. "We can
hear her thoughts!"

I MUST OBEY EFFLUVIA ... BUT I
MISS MY HOME ...

I know how that feels, Emily thought.
She suddenly had an idea. "Can she hear

my thoughts?" she asked.

"We are connected," Marina said. "She might be able to …"

Emily concentrated hard, making her thoughts soothing and calm. She hoped that the squid would understand her.

Hello there! she called to her. Layla, Marina and Grace jumped. Emily stifled a smile. Her friends could hear her thoughts – but could the squid?

I know how you feel, Emily thought. The squid's tentacles slowed. She was listening! Emily thought about how homesick she'd felt in the morning, and how much she'd longed to go home. *I used to feel lost and scared, too. But*

*being somewhere new is exciting. I've
made new friends and gone on an
amazing mermaid adventure! We
want to be your friends and
help you,* she told the
squid. *You don't have
to follow Effluvia.*

As the squid paused, she stopped thrashing. The weird hypnotised light went from her eyes and the seas around her calmed.

"Thank you," the squid said in a deep rumble, "for understanding how I feel. My name is Octavia."

"Whoa!" said Grace, impressed. "It worked, Emily!"

"That was brilliant!" Layla whispered.

Marina grinned. "Emily, that was amazing! You were born to be a mermaid!"

Emily felt herself blushing at the compliments. But then she caught sight of Splash, as he and Kai peeked out

132

nervously from behind the rock.

"We've still got to find Splash's family and get the pearl," she said determinedly. "Effluvia's right, we can't celebrate just yet!" She turned to Kai. "Now that the water's calm can you call the dolphins?"

"No problem," Kai said. "I'll use my sonar."

He let out a chorus of loud clicks. As they waited, Layla stroked Splash comfortingly. "We'll find your mum soon," she promised him.

Octavia made a whimpering noise.

"Don't worry," Emily promised the squid. "We'll help you get home, too. But first we need to find a pearl."

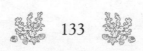

Kai swam around, clicking in all directions. Then suddenly, there was an answering click, and a high-pitched squeal.

"Mama!" Splash said, squirming in Emily's arms. Emily let him go, and the dolphin disappeared behind the rocks.

"Don't get lost again!" Layla called after him.

A few moments later, Splash came back around the rocks, followed by a whole pod of dolphins!

"Oh, thank you, thank you!" cried one of the dolphins, nuzzling Splash. "I'm

Silver, Splash's mum. I was so worried about him – especially when that storm started."

"Oh, sorry, that was me," Octavia said.

The girls quickly explained everything that had happened. The dolphins swam over and crowded around the squid. Soon everyone was talking excitedly, except Grace, who was deep in thought.

"Are you OK?" Emily asked.

Grace nodded. "I'm just thinking – where's Effluvia? Why did she need Octavia to cause the sea storm?"

"Maybe it was just a distraction," said Layla.

"While she looked for the pearl!" Emily

suddenly realised with a gasp.

Grace nodded grimly.

"The seaweed forest isn't too far away,"
said Kai. He pointed with his fin. "It's just
over there."

"That's the way Effluvia went," said
Octavia.

The Sea Keepers exchanged worried looks.

"The clam said the pearl would be gleaming. Effluvia might see it!" Emily said.

"We have to find it before she does!" Layla declared.

"But she's had a head start," said Grace. "We'll never be able to catch up."

The dolphins clicked to each other excitedly. "Maybe we can help," Kai said. "But it might be a wild ride!"

Chapter Nine

"Hold tight to their fins," Marina told the girls, as a dolphin swam up to each of them.

"I'm so going to get seasick!" Layla said, taking hold of Silver's fin.

"I'll try to make it a comfortable ride," Silver told her.

"Don't worry about me," Grace told her dolphin, who was called Saltspray.

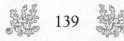

"I love going fast."

Emily felt a thrill of excitement as she reached out and touched her dolphin's smooth skin.

"Hi, I'm Finn," said the dolphin.

Emily put one hand on his fin and held on to his flipper with the other.

"When I say go, kick your tail as hard as you can," Finn told her.

Emily nodded and held on tight. Next

to her, Layla had her eyes squeezed shut,
while Grace swished her tail, impatient
to get going.

"Last one there's a sea slug!" Saltspray
said.

"Now!" clicked Finn, and Emily kicked
out as hard as she could. And they were
off, dashing through the water so fast
that bubbles streamed past her face and
whipped her hair out behind her.

"Woooo hooo!" Grace whooped as she and Saltspray sped along, followed by the giant squid.

"Are we nearly there yet?" Layla yelled.

The sea floor below them turned from rocks to a forest of lush seaweed. The kelp reached nearly up to the surface.

"Wow," Emily breathed.

They swam ahead, weaving in and out through the thick fronds. Barely any light from the surface filtered through the dense seaweed, making it dark and a bit spooky.

"How are we ever going to find a pearl in this?" Emily said, peering into the gloom. "The seaweed forest is massive."

"Hang on, I've got an idea," Finn said, swimming higher, up to the very surface. Suddenly the dolphin leapt out of the water and into the sparkling sunshine.

"Whooooppeeee!" Emily cheered in delight.

Finn swam along the surface, giving Emily a good view of everything below her. She looked down at the others, weaving in and out of the tall kelp, as Finn sped them above the weedy water.

"Do you see what you're looking for?" Finn asked her.

"Not yet," replied Emily. It was like looking for a needle in a haystack. The clam's riddle had said something about a human head, but all she could see was seaweed ...

Finn swam on until the kelp parted into a clearing where a shipwreck was lying on its side. It was crumbled and broken, but the figurehead from the front of the

144

ship was still attached – apart from the statue's head, which was lying on the seabed.

"*Where once a human lost her head!*" Emily whispered. This must be where the pearl was hidden!

Emily let go of Finn and flicked her tail, diving down the gap in the tall kelp. The seaweed caught on her arms and tail as she swam but Emily didn't slow down.

"Everyone, over here! Look near the shipwreck," she yelled.

One by one the others appeared from the nearby weeds.

"It's creepy here," said the baby dolphin, eyeing the shipwreck nervously.

"I'm scared."

"Me too," said the giant squid.

Emily was scared too, but she knew she had to be brave. "Marina, you stay here and look after the animals," she told the mermaid. "The three of us will search the shipwreck."

Ignoring her nerves, Emily flicked her tail again and swam into the spooky shipwreck with her friends. Her eyes straining in the dark, she searched for the pearl. It had to be here somewhere!

Inside the wreck, there were broken chairs and tables covered with seaweed and barnacles. The girls swam through the shipwreck, exploring every inch of it. But there was no sign of the pearl anywhere.

"Maybe it's in here!" cried Grace, waving them over to a chest, half buried in the sand. Layla and Emily swam over to dig the chest out of the sand. But to their disappointment, it was empty.

Just as she was about to give up hope, Emily spotted something. A faint golden light was coming from the sand nearby. She raced over and dug though the sand, hardly daring to breathe. As she brushed away the last bit, the glow got stronger. It was the Golden Pearl!

"On a sandy seabed, just like the clam said!" she whispered. Emily reached out her hand to get the pearl – but before she could grab it, something darted in front of her. Fang! The ugly anglerfish opened his jaws and snatched up the pearl in his mouth.

"No!" Layla cried.

Fang darted out of a porthole and disappeared into the seaweed forest, only his light showing though the fronds.

"After that fish!" Grace shouted.

Emily swam into the thick strands of kelp, but the fronds tangled in her hair and her fins, like she was swimming though wet spaghetti.

"He went that way," Octavia told them, pointing a tentacle.

"There!" Layla gestured to Fang's light bobbing amongst the seaweed.

Emily suddenly remembered something she'd once seen on a nature programme about squid. "Hang on – can you squirt ink?" she asked Octavia.

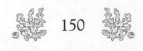

The squid's great eye blinked slowly. "Yes."

"Could you do it now, please? I have an idea ..."

Emily crossed her fingers.

Octavia released a thick cloud of ink over the seaweed. It drifted though the water like a storm cloud, covering the seaweed in inky blackness.

"Please work, please work, please work!" Emily muttered to herself. The forest was now so dark she couldn't even see Fang's light any more.

Suddenly a cry came from the seaweed forest. "Help! Help! I'm scared of the dark!"

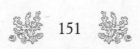

It was Fang!

"Give us the pearl and we'll get you out!" Emily shouted.

"OK!" Fang replied. "But hurry!"

Emily, Layla and Grace rushed over to where they could hear Fang yelping. The squid waved her tentacles over the ink, clearing it just enough for the girls to see the anglerfish. Fang opened his mouth and they saw the faint glow of the pearl as it fell to the seabed. Emily darted forward and grabbed it. The pearl was cool and smooth as she picked it up, and it glowed with golden light.

The anglerfish was shivering with fright, covering his eyes with his fins.

"There you go,"
Layla said kindly,
guiding him up into
the clear water.

Fang turned tail
and sped off into
the ocean, wailing,
"Effluvia! Effluvia!
The human girls have
got the pearl!"

"How did you know
he was afraid of the
dark?" Grace asked.

"I didn't," Emily told
her, "but I guessed –
Fang's always got his

light so he's not used to the dark. And all bullies are cowards."

Laughing, the girls swam to the surface and floated on their backs. After being in the gloomy dark, Emily was happy to feel the sun on her face and the Golden Pearl safely in her hand. They'd done it! They'd saved the seas. Now they really were Sea Keepers.

Chapter Ten

The girls were still basking in the
sunshine when suddenly a horrible laugh
rang out, and Effluvia burst through the
water's surface.

"You didn't think it would be that easy,
did you, Sea Keepers?" she sneered. "As
if your kind could do anything to the
sea except destroy it. Look, see what the
humans bring to the ocean?"

The siren opened her mouth and the girls immediately put their hands over their ears.

"Come to me, a wave of debris,
Left by humans to poison the sea."

There was a rumble and then a huge wave came up behind Effluvia.

"What is that?" Layla whispered.

"Rubbish!" Emily realised with a sinking heart. The wave was full of plastic water bottles, old cartons and tin cans. Once again Emily felt ashamed of the mess humans had made.

The wave grew bigger and bigger until it was a towering tsunami. Effluvia gave a cruel laugh and dropped her hand. The

wave crashed over their heads, pelting
them with all the
rubbish as it went.

Clinging to the
pearl, Emily
dodged and dived
as the rubbish bashed
around her.

"Ouch!" Marina cried out, rubbing her tail where a plastic bottle had hit it.

"Give me that pearl!" Effluvia shrieked.

"Never!" Grace shouted bravely.

Emily held the pearl tightly. This was impossible. Effluvia was never going to stop trying to get a pearl, and one day she might succeed! She thought back to what Marina had said about its power. "We need to use the pearl's magic."

"But aren't we meant to take it back to Atlantis?" Layla said. "We promised."

"We also promised to help mermaid kind," Emily said, thinking about their Sea Keeper vow. "The sea is in grave danger right now! Look at all

158

this rubbish. It could hurt so many sea creatures. We could use the pearl's magic to get rid of it."

"Give me that pearl, two-legs!" Effluvia screeched as she swam towards Emily.

"Quick!" Grace said. "Let's make a wish on the pearl."

Grace and Layla reached out their hands. As soon as all three girls touched the pearl, it was as if time stopped.

"Please," Emily said, "get rid of this rubbish."

The pearl glowed brightly with a gorgeous golden light, then there was a big flash. Emily looked at the pearl in

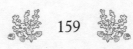
159

her hand. It wasn't golden any more, but white. Its magical power was gone – and so was all of the rubbish!

Effluvia crashed into them, her hand grabbing for the pearl. But when she

 160

saw that its golden glow had vanished she threw it onto the seabed in disgust. "NO!" she shrieked.

"Yes!" Grace yelled, high-finning her friends with her tail. "Sea Keepers one, Effluvia zero!"

Effluvia drew herself up to her full height and thrashed her tail angrily. Grace stopped celebrating and the girls bunched together.

Effluvia's hair floated behind her like an electric blue veil as she glared at them furiously. "You might have found this pearl," she spat, "but I'll get the next one. I only need one to unleash my siren sisters into the oceans and then I'll

rule the waves for ever! And until I do, I'm going to keep stirring up trouble for you Sea Keepers. So don't think you've seen the last of me!"

She grabbed Fang by his light and swam away in a whoosh of water.

There was a stunned silence, and then Marina swam up to them.

"You did it!" she cried excitedly. "You stopped Effluvia!"

The water was calm now, and beautiful, with sunshine glittering above and the fronds of the seaweed forest waving lazily in the tide. Little fish peeked out from among the weeds. There was no sign of rubbish anywhere.

"Do you think it's OK that we used the pearl's magic?" Emily said anxiously.

"I don't know," Marina said. "But we're about to find out ... " She pointed to a small bubble that had appeared in front of her, bobbing up and down insistently.

Marina tapped the bubble and it rippled and grew to the size of a balloon.

Then Queen Adrianna appeared on the bubble's shimmering surface.

"Sea Keepers," the queen said sternly. "We have protected the Golden Pearls for hundreds of years. No mermaid would have ever dared use their magic."

Emily glanced nervously at Layla and Grace. Layla was biting her fingernails and Grace was frowning. They looked as worried as she felt. Had they already failed as Sea Keepers?

"And that is why I must thank you," continued Adrianna.

"Phew!" Layla whispered.

"The seas are in crisis. It was right to use the pearl to clean up the rubbish and stop its magic from falling into the wrong hands," the queen said, her voice softening. "You human girls have done what no mermaid would have. Perhaps that is why you were chosen to be our Sea Keepers. Congratulations to you all. Come home soon, Marina." The queen nodded and the bubble burst with a pop.

"Yay!" Emily, Layla, Grace and Marina all cheered. The dolphin pod swam around them happily and even

Octavia waved her tentacles.

"NOW we can celebrate!" Layla laughed.

After they'd danced around in joy, Grace asked, "What happens next?"

"I suppose we all go home and wait for the Mystic Clam to remember where another pearl is hidden," Marina said, holding up the one they had found. "I can't wait to see the look on Neptune's face when he sees this. Ha!"

"Our pod can take you back home," Silver offered to Octavia. She nodded gratefully.

After they'd said goodbye to the dolphins and squid, Marina took the girls

back home, too. As they swam to the
cove, Emily noticed something. There
were bits of old rope and an anchor on
the sea floor. A plastic bottle floated by.

"Why didn't the pearl work here?" Emily asked Marina.

"One pearl can only do so much. It got rid of the rubbish from Effluvia's tidal wave," explained Marina, "but the oceans are vast and full of so much plastic."

The girls looked at each other sadly as Marina led them up to the surface. They were back in the cave where they'd first met her, Grace's dinghy on the sand where they'd left it.

"We'll help clean up the oceans," Emily promised. "And we'll help find the other pearls."

Layla and Grace nodded.

Marina hugged them all. "I knew I was right to take you to Atlantis," she said. "I'm so glad you were chosen to be Sea Keepers."

"Me too!" Emily said.

"And me!" Grace added.

"Hmmm," Layla pretended to think about it. Grace splashed her with her tail.

"Of course I'm happy about it!" Layla laughed.

The girls swam to the edge of the water. Emily sat on the sand and looked at her tail sparkling in the shallows. She touched her beautiful scales and splashed her fins. She hoped she'd get to be a mermaid again soon!

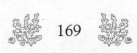

Marina started to sing:

"Water magic, listen to me,
Channel the power of the sea.
Take these girls from water to sand,
Give them their legs to walk on land."

Emily wiggled her fins as they magically turned back into toes.

"Argh, I've got a wet bum!" Layla shrieked. Her dungarees were wet where they'd been sitting in the water.

Emily's jeans and shoes were wet too, but she didn't mind.

"Aw, I miss my tail already," Layla said, standing up.

"Yeah, but now we can do this!" Grace jumped up and did a cartwheel.

Emily stood up and stretched. It was
nice to have her legs back.

Marina laughed
from the water as
Grace did another
cartwheel.

"When will we see
you again?" Emily
asked the mermaid.

"As soon as
the Mystic Clam
remembers where
another pearl
is hidden, your
bracelets will
glow," explained Marina. "To become

a mermaid again, just say these magic
words:

Take me to the ocean blue,
Sea Keepers to the rescue!"

Then Marina waved, and with a flash
of bright hair and sparkling tail, she was
gone.

Chapter Eleven

Emily stared at the aquamarine water. "Did that just really happen?" she wondered out loud.

Grace pushed the dingy off the sand and they all climbed in. "It seems like a beautiful dream," she said.

"But we have our bracelets – and this." Layla pointed to the bottom of the dingy, to the fishing net Kai had been caught in.

Grace started up the dinghy and they sailed out of the cave. Back at the harbour, the fishermen were still unloading their catch, with a familiar ginger cat sitting next to the boat, miaowing hungrily.

"Nemo!" Emily jumped onto the

 harbour wall and rushed over to pick him up. He purred happily as she buried her face in his soft fur. "You'll never guess where I've been," she told him.

Grace and Layla came along behind her, holding the net.

"Awww!" Layla stopped to pet Nemo, who sniffed at the net suspiciously.

But Grace went straight up to a white-haired fisherman "Grandad!" she cried.

"Where did you get that?" he asked, noticing the net.

"A dolphin was trapped in it," Layla explained. She launched into the story of how they'd untangled Kai from the net.

 175

Emily felt a flicker of nerves as she looked at the fishermen, who had gathered around to listen. How could she tell them to stop being careless with their nets? They were grown-ups and she was just a kid. As Nemo purred in her arms, Emily thought about the dolphins and all the other creatures she'd met. They deserved a safe home. And the Sea Keepers had promised to help.

Taking a deep breath, Emily said, "Do you know about ghost nets? They just keep catching fish and killing things, forever."

"They are a big problem," Grace's grandad said, rubbing the back of his

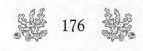 176

neck. He shrugged. "But what can we do? It's the big ships and the plastic companies that are the main problem."

"We have to do *something*," Grace said. Her eyes flashed fiercely and Emily knew that she was thinking about her Sea Keeper promise, too.

"We could start by cleaning up this cove," Emily said.

"This is Emily, her family have just bought the Mermaid café," Grace explained to her grandfather.

"You're right, Emily!" Grace's grandad declared. "We need to do something. *The Salty Seahorse* is not going to fish any more today. Instead, we are going

to clean up our cove!"

"Aye, aye, Captain!" agreed the crew.

"I can't believe we did so much!" Emily said in delight.

The fishermen had dredged lost lobster pots, nets and fishing line from the cove, as well as hundreds of other bits of rubbish. Lots of people had come to see what was happening, and then stayed to help with the beach clean-up.

Emily knew there was still a lot of work to do – but this was a good start.

"The cove looks like we've used another

magic pearl!" Layla joked as they finally
finished for the day.

"Take that, Effluvia!" Grace agreed.

Emily scooped up Nemo from where

 179

he was snoozing in the sunshine and led her new friends back to the café. Dad was unpacking some boxes and Mum was taking a scrummy-looking tray of cakes out of the oven.

"Mum and Dad, meet Layla and Grace," Emily said. "They helped me find Nemo."

"Told you he'd be OK!" Dad said, but he looked relieved too.

"By the way, I'm adopted," Emily said to her new friends. She always felt like she had to explain why she looked so different from her parents.

"Oh!" Layla gasped.

Emily's tummy turned over and she

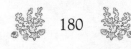

looked at her friend. Did Layla think that was weird?

But Layla had a dreamy look in her eyes and was sniffing the wonderfully chocolatey aroma that filled the cafe. "Oh, *what* is that amazing smell?"

"Mum's famous triple chocolate chunk muffins!" Emily said proudly.

"Mmmmmmm!" Grace sighed.

"You girls can be my official taste testers," Mum said, handing them each a still-warm muffin.

Emily grinned. "I'm going to show Layla and Grace my room, OK?"

Munching the muffins, the girls went up the windy staircase to the tiny but

cosy flat upstairs. Emily's room was still piled with boxes, but Dad had put Nemo's bed in a sunny spot on the window seat. Nemo jumped in and curled up happily. He clearly felt at home already – and so did she, Emily realised with a burst of happiness.

"You can see the sea from your bedroom!" Layla said.

Grace stood on Emily's other side and the three girls looked down at the sparkling sea. Somewhere out there, underneath the waves, were mermaids. And hopefully soon, Emily and her new friends would be joining them again for another mermaid adventure!

The End

Join Emily, Grace and Layla
for another mermaid adventure in …

The Sea Unicorn

"Hey, wait for me!" Layla flicked her aquamarine tail and swam after her mermaid friends. She laughed as she caught up with them and they spun round in a circle …

"Layla! Stop daydreaming!" Grace laughed.

Layla shook her head and looked around. She wasn't underwater, she was in her kitchen, sitting at the table with her best friends with their homework spread out in front of them.

"Were you thinking about the mermaids?" Emily asked.

"Ssssh!" Grace said, looking over at where Layla's dad and her big sister, Nadia, were making dinner.

Luckily, Dad was busy reading the recipe and Nadia had her earphones in. "Oooh yeah, I loooooooveeee you," she sang, jigging about as she chopped an onion.

The girls giggled. Layla beckoned to her friends, and they put their heads so close that Layla's straight, dark hair was almost touching Emily's black curls and Grace's long, blonde hair. "I was thinking about the mermaids," she whispered. "I wish our bracelets would glow so we could visit them again!" Layla didn't just daydream about mermaids, she really did have adventures with them!

It had all started when she, Emily and Grace had rescued a dolphin called Kai, who had turned out to be the pet of Marina, a mermaid princess. Marina was the coolest person Layla had ever met. She had taken the girls to her palace in the incredible underwater kingdom of Atlantis. There, to everyone's surprise, Layla, Grace and Emily had been chosen to become Sea Keepers – the only ones who could find the Golden Pearls

and save Atlantis from the evil Siren,
Effluvia. Ever since they had got back
home, the three friends had been waiting
for the magic bracelets Marina had given
them to glow and take them on another
mermaid adventure!

"You're daydreaming again!" Grace said.

Layla stuck her tongue out at her friend.

"Come on," Emily told them, "we've
got to work out what we're going to do
for our project!"

Layla gave a dramatic sigh, but she
picked up the homework sheet and tried
to read what it said. There were some
really long words.

"OK, so maybe we could do a poster, or

a presentation—" Grace started.

"Wait a second," Layla told her, frowning as she concentrated on the words.

"Oh, sorry," Grace said. "I forgot."

"What's wrong?" Emily asked.

Sometimes Layla forgot that she hadn't known Emily that long because she had only moved to their seaside town recently. "It takes me a bit longer because I've got dyslexia," she explained. "The letters get muddled. But I'm good at other things – like solving problems."

"Do you want me to read it for you?" Emily offered.

Layla shook her head. "I can do it," she said, breaking the tricky words into smaller parts. "Around the world, chil-dren have been going on strike from school to pro-test about glo-bal warming," she read. "Make a project to tell people about en-vi-ron-men-tal cha-llen-ges. Be im-a-gin-a-tive."

Read **The Sea Unicorn** to find out what happens next!

How to be a real-life

Would you like to be a Sea Keeper just like Emily, Grace and Layla? Here are a few ideas for how you can help protect our oceans.

1. Try to use less water
Using too much water is wasteful. Turn off the tap when you brush your teeth and take shorter showers.

2. Use fewer plastic products
Plastic ends up in the ocean and can cause problems for marine wildlife. Instead of using plastic bottles, refill a metal bottle. Carry a tote bag when out shopping, and use non-disposable food containers and cutlery.

Sea Keeper

3. Help at a beach clean-up

Keeping the shore clear of litter means less litter is swept into the sea. Next time you're at the beach or a lake, try and pick up all the litter you can see.

4. Reduce your energy consumption

Turn off lights when you aren't using a room. Walk or cycle instead of driving. Take the stairs instead of the lift. Using less energy helps reduce the effects of climate change.

5. Avoid products that harm marine life

Do not buy items made from endangered species. If you eat seafood, make sure it comes from sustainable sources.

Dive in to a mermaid adventure!

The Sea Unicorn
Coral Ripley

Coral Reef Rescue
Coral Ripley

Sea Turtle School
Coral Ripley

Penguin Island
Coral Ripley

Coming Soon